Elephi Pelephi
Well-Known Cat Formerly Kitten

Elephi

THE CAT WITH THE HIGH IQ

Jean Stafford

Illustrated by Erik Blegvad

Dover Publications, Inc.
Mineola, New York

For Jeannie and Joey Charoux

Bibliographical Note

Elephi: The Cat with the High IQ, first published by Dover Publications, Inc.,
in 2017, is an unabridged republication of the work originally published by Dell
Publishing Co., Inc., New York, in 1962. An illustration by Erik Blegvad that did
not appear in the original publication is included on the inside covers of this
Dover edition.

International Standard Book Number

ISBN-13: 978-0-486-81426-1
ISBN-10: 0-486-81426-2

Elephi Pelephi Well-Known Cat Formerly Kitten sat in the bay window watching the snow. He was alone and he was lonesome. Mr. and Mrs. Cuckoo, with whom he shared his apartment, were both out. Mr. Cuckoo was at his rare book shop and Mrs. Cuckoo was at the ten cent store buying Christmas wrappings and ribbon.

Earlier, Elephi had sat on the top of a chest of drawers supervising Madella, who ran the vacuum cleaner, as she got ready to go home. She put on her green coat and her green hat with a feather in it, her woolly taffy-colored scarf and her fleece-lined boots and then she pulled the string that turned out the light in the back hall. She said, "You be good, hear? Bye-bye, Elephi, see you tomorrow." And she was gone.

The first thing Elephi did as soon as the door was closed was to leap up and catch the end of the string and turn the light on again.

After that, he moseyed into the kitchen and nibbled at the leaves of the sweet-potato vine in the window sill. He jumped into the sink and caught a drop of water from the faucet with his tongue. He opened a cupboard door and pulled out a roll of paper towels which he unrolled like a carpet, a bumpy and unfinished-looking carpet, to be sure, but better than none.

Then he went into the bathroom and arranged himself in the wash basin for a nap (it was exactly the right shape for the Curled Cat position—paws tucked in, tip of tail touching tip of nose) but he found that he wasn't sleepy.

So he made a tour of the dining room where he found his own personal walnut. He played hockey with it until it hid.

Next he went into the living room to look through the window at the children leaving the nursery school at the Presbyterian church across the street. They were all bundled up in red snow suits and mittens and peaked hoods and they made noises like birds as they trudged through the snow with their mothers.

When the last child disappeared, there was nothing left for Elephi to do but watch the gentle snowflakes whirling and twirling among the spires of the church and the tops of the bare trees. He grew thoughtful.

He wished he had a friend near his own age,

a cat or a boy or a horse. He liked the Cuckoos, but they were old enough to be his great-grand-parents, *more* than old enough. And, also, they were cuckoo.

Their name was really Moneypenny, but he called them Cuckoo because that's what they were. To begin with, they had given him such a silly name, Elephi. Who in the wide world ever heard of a cat named Elephi? The Cuckoos claimed they did. They said they had met a marmalade tom by that name at a hotel in Delphi in Greece and had become good friends with him. (This cat had loved potato chips and goat cheese.) That was all very well except that Elephi II was an American, born in New York City, of parents whose families had been in this country for thousands of generations. Indeed, one of his ancestors, Felix Oglethorpe by name, had been Mouser-in-Chief for George Washington's barn at Mount Vernon. If Elephi had been naming himself, he would have picked something made in the U.S.A., some-thing like Bill or O'Reilly or Huckleberry. Moreover, he didn't look anything at all like that foreign orange cat, for he wore a formal black suit with a white shirt and white underclothes and short white gloves. His whiskers were long and his large eyes were very dark.

His full name, Elephi Pelephi Well-Known Cat Formerly Kitten, had been given to him when he came of age on his first birthday, December 15, just a week ago. He understood the Formerly Kitten part of it because, of course, he was grown up, but he was not Well-Known and he knew he wasn't. His name wasn't even listed in the telephone directory nor had it ever appeared in the *Daily News*.

All the same, his birthday party had been so much fun that he didn't begrudge the Cuckoos this particular cuckooness. They had given him a felt sombrero filled with catnip, a ball with a jingle bell inside, and a green rubber mouse. He had chicken for dinner. All evening, after he had chewed up the hat and had lost the ball with the bell and had cornered the mouse under a footstool, the Cuckoos played with him. They threw corks and wadded-up paper for him to fetch and bring back to them. Friends

of the Cuckoos said he must have learned this trick of retrieving from a hunting dog, but he hadn't. He had been born knowing a great many useful things. For instance, he had been

turning the back hall light off and on ever
since he was a mere baby. And anyhow, he
didn't know any dogs and didn't think he
wanted to. Often he watched the poodles and

dachshunds of the neighborhood out on their walks up and down Fifth Avenue and he thought they were a clumsy lot. Clumsy, and show-offs too, with their vulgar barking and their noisy threats to eat each other up.

Oh, he had really nothing to complain about, Elephi told himself as he sat there watching the snow. For one thing, he wasn't a dog.

And the apartment was big and it had plenty of high places to jump to—bookcases, mantel-pieces, china closets. And places to hide—spaces back of desks and under chairs and behind books and inside the umbrella stand. There were ferns and geraniums to pounce at and window shades to yank up and curtain pulls to be used as punching bags. There were countless objects to be pushed off tables: letter openers, paperweights, a marble egg, ash trays, two birds made of cow horn, three giraffes made of wood, a silver pig, a copper sheep bell. When he wanted to see how good looking he was, there were mirrors all over the place to show him to himself. Then, besides the wash basin, there were other excellent beds under lamps, on radiators, on a camel saddle (why the Cuckoos thought they needed a camel saddle on lower Fifth Avenue, he could not imagine, but there it was in the living room), in a laundry basket, and in a wooden salad bowl.

On the whole, the food was good, and there was plenty of it. He had an egg yolk for breakfast to keep his clothes shiny, and for dinner he sometimes had liver (that was lovely) and sometimes kidney (very nice too—chewy, you know) and sometimes codfish (this was the best of all) and sometimes a kind of hash out of a can (filling but not much fun) and once in a great while (as on his birthday) beautiful chicken.

Elephi did not drink water or milk in the usual way out of a saucer. Instead, he dipped his front paws, first one and then the other, into a glass or a cream pitcher and licked off the liquid. It tasted twice as good that way. In a manner of speaking, he quenched his thirst and washed his feet at the same time.

He had a good life, he admitted. All the same, it would be a much better one if there

11

was somebody young in the house to keep him company. What grand times he could have if there was another cat to wrestle with! They could have races up and down the long halls and hurdle-jumping in the living room, using the chairs and sofas as obstacles. They could have boxing matches and games of hide-and-seek, Cops and Robbers, Run Sheep Run. He sighed, feeling underprivileged.

Elephi Pelephi Well-Known Cat Formerly Kitten sighed again and started to close his eyes in sorrow. But just then the mounted police-men came down Fifth Avenue on their way to the stable. Every day at this same time they passed in front of the church and Elephi loved to watch the proud, official horses. Today great clouds of steam came out of their noses and their riders, the policemen, were red and blue in the face from the cold.

By now the streets were slick with snow and the taxicabs and the lubberly busses swerved and zigzagged and grumbled and groaned. The wind had come up and as Elephi watched, it turned a blue umbrella inside out. The lady who had been under it looked puzzled, as if to say, "What do you do with an inside-out umbrella?" Finally she stuck it in the rubbish basket on the corner and it looked ridiculous. It looked like somebody with a dozen legs who had fallen headlong into the basket and couldn't get out.

A small white car that had been creeping down the Avenue began to skid. It skidded around the corner into the side street by the entrance to the nursery school and there it stopped. Elephi could hear it trying to start again. The noise it made was a cross between a scream and a moan with a whimper in the middle, a most mournful sound. Its rear wheels spun wildly, churning up the snow, and the faster the wheels went, the more woebegone grew the cry. But it was plainly stuck for good, poor thing; it could not have budged if its life depended on it. Elephi would not have felt so sorry if the car had not been so extremely small. It was no longer than a bathtub and not much taller.

Presently the left-hand door of the car was

13

flung open and out got a perfectly enormous man wearing a perfectly enormous raccoon coat. Not only was he remarkably fat but he was also so tall that his head must have been pressed against the top of the car. There couldn't have been room for anything else except him on the front seat, not so much as a piece of paper or a toothpick. It was as if a hippopotamus had got into the Cuckoos' bath-

tub. He must have been very uncomfortable, thought Elephi. But the car must have been quite as uncomfortable. A man of that size and shape had no right to drive an automobile designed for somebody eight or nine years old. Elephi growled indignantly, taking sides with the car. The man wore a black beard, too, and his face was red with wrath. He called the car dreadful names. He opened up its mouth and looked inside and hollered worse ones.

The awful brute slapped the car and he kicked it and then he went flouncing down the street, looking back every now and again, shouting and shaking his fist.

What a cad!

The car sat there, silent and motionless, tired to death. The snow piled up thickly around its wheels. The wind wailed and the sky began to darken and Elephi shivered although his coat was warm. He hoped that help would come for the car before night fell. It would be scary for it to be forsaken in the storm.

But no one came. The street lights flashed on

and so did the cheerful red and green lights on the Christmas trees in the church yard. The snow circled clockwise and then counterclockwise and it put a hat on the white car's head and a smothering mask on its nose. Soon, if this kept up, the car would be buried alive.

Usually when Elephi heard the Cuckoos at the door, he went into the hall to greet them. But today when Mrs. Cuckoo came in, he was still in the bay window, and it wasn't until she had turned on the lamps and called, "Cat? Oh, cat, cat, where are you?" that he jumped down and went to welcome her and make her feel at home.

For five or ten minutes he was distracted from the plight of the car as he helped Mrs. Cuckoo undo her bundles. He carried some of the string into the bedroom and some of it into the bathroom. He tore up the cellophane and put bits of it in handy places. And then he got into a brown paper bag that she had emptied and clawed his way through the bottom of it.

17

He could much more easily have got out of it the way he had entered, but that would have been a lazy thing to do.

By and by Elephi went back to the window. The car was still there and now it looked like a solid hill of snow.

Mrs. Cuckoo went into the kitchen and found the paper towel rug and she cried, "Elephi Pelephi! I declare I have never in all my live-long days known anyone more vexatious. Come here this minute!" Everyone knows that cats don't take orders. (Another advantage in being a cat, thought Elephi. Dogs had to "Get off the sofa!" "Heel!" "Sit!" whereas cats did what they wanted when they wanted and took their own sweet time.) Mrs. Cuckoo came into the living room and scratched him behind the ears.

"Villainous witch's companion," she said, massaging his shoulders. "Why aren't you purring, Pelephi El? And what *are* you looking at?" He would have been glad to tell her if he had known how, and she might have rescued the car in some way or other. But all he could do was to look up into her face and meow.

18

Mrs. Cuckoo turned on the radio and the weather man said that there were already fifteen inches of snow and there was no relief in sight. It was going to be very cold, the man said, and the wind was from the west at forty miles an hour. Suddenly Elephi howled. He couldn't help it. His mouth opened of its own accord and an amazing howl came out. Mrs. Cuckoo snapped off the radio and looked at him closely.

"What is your problem, my dear friend?" she asked him earnestly. "Are you hungry? Or are you sick?" and in reply, he howled again. He began to shudder and he jumped down from the window seat, ran across the room, leaped onto a table and assumed the Curled Cat position around the base of a lamp. What if *he* were out in the snow, deserted by his friends? The look of the cold car had made him feel as if his own bones had turned to icicles.

"A penny . . . or rather, a million dollars for your secret thoughts," said Mrs. Cuckoo and stroked his head-bone fondly. "Howl like a monster one minute, purr like an angel the next. You make no sense." She shrugged her shoulders and went into the kitchen to cook Mr. Cuckoo's dinner.

Elephi, the Prominent Cat of 43 Fifth Avenue, wanted very much to go to sleep and dream about the springtime when the Presbyterians' trees were in leaf and the Cuckoos bought armloads of lilacs from the Italian man with the pushcart. He wanted to sleep and dream so that he could forget about the car and how cold it was. But he was wide awake. He changed his position and moved some of Mr. Cuckoo's rare books that were in his way. He stretched. He yawned. He counted mice. But he could not go to sleep.

"Rats!" said restless Elephi.

If there were only some way to get out of the apartment, and out of the building, and across the street, he might be able to tunnel a passage through the snowdrifts and somehow get into the car—he was clever at opening doors if they weren't locked. He would warm the inside of the car and purr to it. Or, rather, purr to *him*, for now he thought of the car as Whitey, the

Orphan of the Storm. And he would remain there, purring, until somebody came to take the poor waif home.

But, alas, Elephi P. Cat was not allowed out of the apartment because the Cuckoos had an idea that he might go travelling and get lost in Brooklyn or in the Radio City Music Hall. Or that he might be catnapped by a treacherous furrier who took a fancy to his elegant suit. Once, when the laundry man came and dawdled (he was making eyes at Madella who was far more beautiful than any movie star or royal queen) the brave and self-sufficient hero of this story managed to get out into the public hall, which was full of mysterious and interesting shadows and smells. But Madella, helped by the laundry man (he was a dope) caught him just as he was about to explore the stairs going down.

What a nice, sympathetic cat he was to fret so about a small white car that he didn't even know! He gave up trying to sleep.

He jumped from the table to a lower table where he found an open package of cigarettes.

Neatly he removed the cigarettes and put claw-holes in all of them so that they couldn't be smoked. He did this partly for fun and partly because in his opinion the Cuckoos smoked too much.

Throughout the evening, Elephi kept returning to his post in the bay window to watch Whitey disappear.

He performed his chores as usual, but his heart was not in his work. When Mrs. Cuckoo set the table for dinner, he pushed off the knives and unfolded the napkins and scooped the salt out of the salt dishes. And when Mr. Cuckoo came home and started to read the news, he charged the paper and sat down on the editorial page. Mr. Cuckoo said, "Listen, you, if it weren't for herself and the dinner herself is making me, I'd have you up on a charge of disturbing the peace. If there's one thing I hate more than another it's a black cat sitting on my editorial page." And old man Cuckoo handed him his thumb to box.

Elephi emptied the ice bucket onto the rug

and he put Mr. Cuckoo's gloves in a safe place under a chair which had a skirt that went down to the floor. He renewed his acquaintance with the rubber birthday mouse who happened to be under the same chair.

But Elephi was absent-minded and sad.

Mrs. Cuckoo said, "The Well-Known Cat has something on his mind. I think he wants a chum."

And Mr. Cuckoo said, "This steak is a miracle. He doesn't need a chum. He's got *you*, hasn't he?"

"Yes," said Mrs. Cuckoo, "but sometimes I think he'd like a non-human being around the house."

Mr. Cuckoo said, "Give me some more steak."

So Mrs. Cuckoo knew that Elephi was lonesome. Maybe she would do something about it.

The Well-Known Cat did not sleep well that night. He would wake up from a bad dream and look out the window. And the snow never stopped and the wind wailed and whistled and

yelped and whinnied. It rattled the window-panes and it bent the Presbyterian trees. There were cars stalled everywhere. Some of them had been left in the middle of the street and at catty-cornered angles. It looked rather as if they had all started to play a game but had forgotten the rules so that everything had ended up in confusion.

But the other cars were bigger than Whitey and none was so completely covered up. Cat imagined that they were bored and unhappy, but he did not really worry about them: Whitey was the original Orphan of the Storm.

At about noon the next day the snow finally stopped, and Elephi grew even more restless, waiting for Whitey's horrid guardian to come and dig him out. He was afraid that the bearded giant would give the car a scolding, but all the same would take him home to his warm garage.

Hours passed.

Nobody came.

Pedestrians made their way around Whitey and laughed at him. A policeman came and pushed away just enough snow to put a ticket on his windshield and when Madella saw this, she said to Mrs. Cuckoo, "There's one car that'll wind up in the car pound and that's for sure."

Car pound! Elephi had heard about the dog pound which he gathered was a kind of reform school, and he supposed a car pound was much the same thing. It seemed highly unfair since Whitey had done nothing criminal—he had simply been too tired and cold to carry that big fat drip with the whiskers one more step.

There must be a way to save Whitey from the car pound. But though Elephi, who had a very high I.Q., thought and thought, he could not make a plan.

Several days passed. It was sunny and the snow glittered like precious gems and it was wickedly cold. The Presbyterian children made a snow man in the church yard, and the older boys of the neighborhood had terrific snowball fights. Gradually some of the cars were dug out and warmed up and coaxed away.

Not Whitey. His cap of snow grew dirty but it did not melt. He was encased in such tight-packed snow that the snowball fighters climbed on top of him and slid down and probably did not even know that there was a car inside that great hump.

Elephi, the Compassionate Cat, lost his appetite. He slept less than twenty hours out of each twenty four. He grew careless in his personal appearance and seldom laundered his gloves. When company came to see the Cuckoos, he was polite, but after he had been introduced, he begged to be excused and returned to his bay window. Madella, seeing that this was now his favorite spot, put a bright red cushion on the window seat and here he sat, like a king on a throne, hour after hour, thinking and thinking of a way to rescue Whitey.

On one of these cold, sparkling days, the smart cat had an idea. Whitey was so small that he could easily be brought into the building and into the back elevator. The Cuckoos' back door was rather narrow, but with a little juggling and jiggling, it could be managed to get the car through and into the room at the end of the hall where the ironing board and brooms were kept. Here Whitey could stay and Well Known could take care of him. He probably needed a good bath by this time. But above all, he needed warmth and friendship.

The Former Kitten began to plot. His problem was a tough one and a less clever cat would have thrown up his paws in dismay. But not Elephi Moneypenny. He put on his thinking cap and thought so hard that Mrs. Cuckoo had to speak to him three times before he realized that she was inviting him to have a snack of chicken.

A big box had come for the Cuckoos several days before and there was a tag on it that gave their name and address and the warning DO NOT OPEN UNTIL CHRISTMAS. It was a matter of only half an hour or so before Elephi had untied the tag and hidden it in his office under the sofa. (The office contained his many safe-deposit boxes where he kept cellophane, corks and perforated cigarettes.)

After hiding the tag, Elephi lay down on his regal red cushion in the window seat. Although he appeared to be asleep, he was really waiting for his chance to get out to the street, across it, and onto the car. He knew exactly what he was going to do if he had any kind of luck.

And he *did* have luck. Absolutely marvelous luck. Lady Luck her very own self smiled on Elephi II. Both door bells rang at once. Madella went to the back door and Mrs. Cuckoo went to the front door and just as she opened it, the telephone rang. She said to the delivery man, "Come in. Just let me get the telephone and I'll be with you in a minute."

The delivery man had several parcels and he propped the door open with one of them while he went to get the others from the elevator. Before you could say, "Electric eel!" Elephi had picked up his DO NOT OPEN sign in his teeth and had run out the door.

"Hey!" called the delivery man. "Hey! Hey, ma'am, is it all right if your cat gets out?"

Elephi, running down the stairs as fast as he could, heard Mrs. Cuckoo cry, "What? What about my cat?"

"It got out," said the delivery man. (*It*, indeed!)

"Oh, no!" Mrs. Cuckoo shrieked. "Madella! Elephi got out! Call Walter! Run and get your snow boots on and I will too!"

Walter, the superintendent, was a nice man but he was big and fat and slow on his feet and Elephi knew that he could easily outrun him.

For one moment, the Cat Formerly Kitten paused, feeling sorry for Mrs. Cuckoo. There was no way of telling the old dear that he was coming right back, so he ran on, and in no time he was in the lobby. A great many people were coming in and going out and Elephi had no trouble slipping through the two heavy outer doors.

Now, for the first time in his life, he found himself on the street.

How huge the world was! And how noisy! And how *cold!* He had been wondering for some time now what snow felt like, and to his surprise and delight, he found it quite similar to a pillow. It was more slippery and, of course, much colder, but it had a kind of bounciness

about it that he liked. And if he had not had business to attend to, he might have tried a sample nap on a mound of it at the curb.

But he was a cat with a purpose and he went directly across the street, crossing with the green light (since he had spent so much time watching the traffic, he knew all the laws) and he leaped nimbly onto the top of Whitey's head. He put down his tag for a minute while he removed the policeman's rude one and buried it in the snow cap. Then, using his teeth and his claws and all his strength and his high I.Q. (if Elephi had been a boy, he probably would have been rated "genius"), he put his own tag on the windshield under the windshield wiper.

The brilliant cat then sat down to wait for the rescue party to come and rescue *him*.

Walter came charging out of the apartment house like a fireman, moving faster than Elephi ever dreamed he could. Big as he was (his hands were like roasts of beef) he was ever so gentle and with the softest voice in the world, he called, "Kitty, kitty, here, kitty, here Mis'

Moneypenny's black kitty!" Elephi would have liked to tease Walter by hiding, and he rather wished his clothes were white so that he wouldn't show up so clearly against the snow. But he wanted to get Whitey into the house as soon as possible and to do this, he had to make Walter look at the tag. So he stayed where he was and Walter spotted him at once.

"Now why'd you want to go and do a thing like that for?" said Walter, reaching up one of his big hands to grab the runaway. "Who you think gonna give you fish and fixins if you go turn into a common low-class bum. Scarin' your missus. The idea! You come along home now, hear?"

Elephi moved just out of Walter's reach and then, when one white-gloved paw was dangling over the DO NOT OPEN tag, he let Walter pick him up.

"Le's see," said Walter. "Le's see, what's this?" and he looked at the tag. "Now what kind of a monkeyshine is this here?" he said, puzzled. "It sure says Moneypenny."

Elephi mewed. He was afraid Mrs. Cuckoo

would come out of the house and discover the tag and catch him red-handed in his trick. So he mewed again more loudly.

"Okay, Mister," said Walter. "I'll get you safe back in your house and then I'll come and take a look at this other matter."

Just as they crossed the street, Mrs. Cuckoo came flying down the steps with one foot in a snow boot and the other in a bedroom slipper. Elephi changed hands and Mrs. Cuckoo said, "Walter, how can I thank you? I don't know what I'd do if anything happened to this ungrateful party!" To Elephi she said, "You're about as bad as a cat can be and still be a cat."

Walter pushed his cap back and scratched his forehead and he said, "Something mighty funny over yonder . . ."

But he did not have a chance to finish because Elephi began to squirm and Mrs. Cuckoo said, "I'll see you later, Walter. Right now I want to get this animal under lock and key."

His mission was accomplished and Elephi lay quietly in Mrs. Cuckoo's arms and purred as she took him up in the elevator. Madella, wearing boots and a scarf around her head, was coming out the door and Elephi mewed a friendly hello to her.

"Well!" she said. "You just wanted to go and do your Christmas shopping, didn't you, Your Highness? What were you going to get me?"

"Don't be nice to him, Madella," said Mrs. Cuckoo. "His sole solitary purpose in running away was to scare the living daylights out of me."

If Elephi had known how to laugh, he would have laughed his head off thinking about the success of his project. But since he couldn't laugh, he purred and this he did with so much power that Madella said he sounded like the BMT subway.

As soon as the ladies finished petting him and observing to each other that he was the best but the most bothersome of cats, Elephi went to his window. Sure enough, Walter was back across the street, brushing snow off Whitey's windshield. Now and again he would stop and scratch his head and shrug his shoulders as if to say, "It sure beats me." After a

35

while, he came back to the building and soon went out again carrying a shovel. Elephi's heart thumped and bumbled like a June-bug.

Walter began to dig. First he dug out the wheels and then he started on the top. The snow had turned to ice and he had to chip it away with a trowel. Elephi was sorry that Walter had such a tiresome job to do. Still, somebody had to do it and Elephi knew that he, personally, could not. His claws were long and strong (the Cuckoos' furniture showed evidence of that) but they were not *that* long and strong.

Walter would stop for a bit to rest. Sometimes he came back across the street and vanished into the building and Elephi imagined that he was getting a cup of hot coffee to warm him up.

Madella put away the vacuum cleaner and dried the last dish and went home. And soon after that, Mrs. Cuckoo went out, telling Elephi that she was going to the dentist. There—that was one more fine thing about being a cat: you didn't have to go to the dentist. Poor cuckoo old Mrs. Cuckoo, she was forever and a day going to the dentist. She would come home from a session with him and vow that she would never go back again. And Mr. Cuckoo would tell her that he didn't want to see her wearing store-teeth quite yet. "But it hurts," she would complain. Nevertheless, she always kept her appointment and when she came home from it, she would lay her cheek on Elephi's flank and say, "A cat is a peerless poultice."

Before leaving, Mrs. Cuckoo hemmed and hawed. "Why don't I call and tell him my cat's sick?" she said and started to the telephone. But she already had on her coat and her boots and she thought the better of it and said, "Okay, Dr. Dreado, just this one more time." And she left.

Now Elephi was alone. But, he thought joyfully, not for long.

A good deal of Whitey had become visible and Elephi could see that he was truly so small that he looked rather like a large toy. Walter worked away: dig, shovel, chip. Sam, the handyman, who was shorter and thinner than Walter and somewhat resembled a kindly mouse, came to help with another shovel and long before the sun went down and long before the Cuckoos came home, Whitey, the Orphan of the Storm, was rid of his winter overcoat of dirty snow.

Not only that! Whitey was actually in the Cuckoos' apartment! In the back room where the ironing board and brooms were! Walter and Sam had put him on a dolly (not the kind of dolly that girls make dresses and aprons for but the kind the Red Cap puts your foot locker and suitcases on when you're catching a train) and wheeled him across Fifth Avenue.

Elephi went to the back door and listened and soon he heard the service elevator coming up with the groan it always made as if it were much too old to do such hard work. He heard Sam say, "Easy, now, easy! Right-o, there we are. I've got the master key right here."

The Well-Known Cat trotted back to the living room, got on his red throne and pretended to be asleep. He heard the two men put Whitey in the back room and he heard Sam say, "I wouldn't mind if somebody gave *me* a little outfit like this for Christmas."

Walter said, "I'd rather have me a Cadillac," and both of them laughed.

"I'll take a look at the plants while I'm here," said Sam and he and Walter came into the living room. Sam and Mrs. Cuckoo often had long conversations about the care and feeding of house plants, and now he felt the leaves of the rubber tree and he prodded the soil in the fern's pot, he pulled a yellow leaf off the pothos and he admired the flaming red blossoms on the amaryllis that had just come into bloom.

Elephi liked both Walter and Sam but today he wished they would go away.

"That's a good-looking cat the Moneypennies got there," said Sam and rolled Elephi over and scratched his stomach. Elephi refused to respond and kept his eyes shut tight.

"You know that big old cat of mine?" said Walter. "Well, I'm gonna get him a monkey to keep him company. I got this squirrel monkey all picked out at the pet store."

How thoughtful of Walter! Why didn't the Cuckoos show their affection for Elephi in the same way? A monkey would be grand.

Sam laughed. "If you're gonna get a monkey to keep your cat company, you better start looking for a new wife to keep *you* company."

"No sir," said Walter. "Bella likes animals. We got the cat and we got the two doves and the dog and the hamsters. She'd like to have a mouse or two."

"Then if you got all them, what do you want with a monkey?" asked Sam.

"Like I said, to keep the cat company. The cat don't like the dog and the doves don't like the cat and the hamsters don't like nobody. The cat's been looking peaked lately and acting mopey, so I figure he needs a friend."

Although Elephi was interested in big, slow Walter's generosity to his cat, he did wish they'd go. Finally, when at last they did, he jumped down immediately and ran like a race horse to the back room.

He stood in the doorway for a few minutes

and purred soothingly and when he spoke, it was in a soft voice so that he would not startle Whitey. He said, "Hello, Car. I'm Elephi."

The car shook and from somewhere deep inside it came a shrill, terrified voice. "An elephant! For Pete's sake, go away. I've had enough trouble as it is without being stepped on by a great lout of an elephant."

"No, no, I'm not an elephant. I'm a cat," said Elephi.

"Then why didn't you say so in the first place? What's the big idea of making a fellow think he was going to have to bunk with an elephant?" said Whitey crossly. "Come around here and let me see if you're telling the truth."

"Where do you want me to stand?" asked Elephi because he was not sure where the car did its looking from.

"In front of my eyes, of course, stupid," said Whitey.

Never before in his life had Elephi been called stupid and he didn't like it in the least. Maybe Whitey was not going to be fun after all.

All the same, he went nearer to the car. At first he stood in front of the head-lights, but this was the wrong place, for Whitey said, "What are you waiting for? I'll bet you're not a cat."

Good heavens, what a peevish car! But Elephi supposed that he would be out of sorts too if he'd been left in the cold snow all that time. He jumped up onto Whitey's hood and stood before the windshield.

This was the right place. Whitey said, "So you are a cat. You're taller than the one at home. And black. The one at home is yellow. Goes by the name of Dandy Lion, King of Beasts."

"I'm Elephi," said Elephi.

"Oh, go on," said Whitey. "If you're an elephant, I'm a Fifth Avenue bus."

"I didn't say I was an elephant," said Elephi. "I said my name is *Elephi*."

"Elephi," said Whitey and thought the news over for a while. "I've heard some strange ones in my time but Elephi is a new one to me. What does it mean?"

"I don't think it *means* anything," said Elephi Pelephi W.K. Cat. "Any more than Susan or Adam or What-you-may-call-it means anything. I'm named for a famous Greek cat of Delphi. The Cuckoos, who pay rent here, tell

43

me that Elephi of Delphi is one of the most important cats in the Mediterranean."

"Never heard of him," said Whitey. Then, in a much friendlier voice, he said, "By the way, Elephi, do you happen to know what language we're speaking? It can't be my native Fiat Italian because you wouldn't understand it, would you?"

"I was wondering about that myself," Elephi replied. "I thought I was speaking American Short-Hair Catese as I usually do, but you wouldn't understand that either, would you?"

"I picked up a few words of Catese from Dandy Lion," said Whitey. "But not much more than 'How do you do?' and 'Move over, please.' Dandy doesn't talk much for the simple reason that he doesn't have much to say. He's nice enough, but between you and me, he hasn't got the brains of a potato."

"It is well known that I have a very high I.Q.," said Elephi.

"So have I!" said Whitey enthusiastically. "You know what I think? I think we're so smart that we have invented an international language without even trying."

"I think you're probably right," said Elephi. "And if that's true, we're smart enough to do anything we want. We could go to the moon if we chose."

"It might be cold at this time of year," said Whitey.

"Yes, I daresay it would be cold right now," said Elephi. "But perhaps we could go in the spring. Listen, Whitey . . ."

"How did you know my name was Whitey?" asked the car.

"It's painted all over you," said Elephi and grinned at his joke.

"If I had a hat, I'd take it off to you," said the little Italian and he sang a song he had just made up.

> "I'd doff my hat
> To the I.Q. cat.
> If I knew Greek, I'd shriek in Greek:
> *Hurrah for Elephi!*"

"Thank you," said Elephi modestly. He curled up companionably on Whitey's hood and he said, "Would you like to tell me the story of your life?"

There was a catch in Whitey's voice as if he were holding back the tears. "It's a story of ups and downs," he said.

Sadly he told it.

Whitey had been taken as an infant from a foundling hospital on Long Island called the Imported Motor Corporation of America. His foster parents, the Blasters, had adopted him to transport their daughter, Miss Alice, from home to her college classes and back. Miss Alice, who was eighteen years old and as pretty as a spring garden in bloom, knew exactly what a small car of Italian parentage liked and what it didn't like. She bathed Whitey often and never let him get tired or overheated and she regularly took him to the clinic for a check-up.

But life with Miss Alice was not entirely a bed of roses. Also living in the Blasters' garage was a big, bossy Cadillac who was always bragging about how strong he was and how fast he could run and how expensive his upholstery was. He sneered at Whitey, called him "shrimp" or "peanut" or "microbe." He would say things like, "Who could have dreamed that I would share a roof with a shrimp? And a foreign shrimp at that?"

Whitey never answered back. It would be a waste of breath to talk to such a blow-hard.

Mr. Blaster (his name suited him to a T) was not nice. He loved his daughter but he thought her taste in cars was silly and he never came into the garage without making a slighting remark much in the manner of the Cadillac. "Looks like a bug from the moon," he would say. Or, "It'll be ready for the dump in a year."

One day not long ago, old Smarty Pants Cadillac came down with a head cold and he refused to go out into the snow. He coughed and sneezed and carried on at a great rate and he told Whitey that he hated to get his tires wet. He said wet tires were undignified to a Cadillac.

So Whitey had to take Mr. Blaster to his office. As he was leaving the garage, the lousy Cadillac laughed rudely and said, "The old man'd better get a horse."

The Blasters lived in Westchester, a long way from Wall Street and Whitey did not look forward to the trip. He would gladly have taken Miss Alice anywhere in any kind of

weather, but traveling with her father was a
horse of a different color. It was like hauling a
load of cement and lead pipes with a few
whales thrown in for good measure. And although Whitey did not complain once about
the snow that blinded him and often made him
skid off the road, and even though he ran as
fast and smoothly as he could under the cir-

cumstances, Mr. Blaster wasn't satisfied. He called Whitey a flop and a dope and a drip and a jellyfish and a watch fob. On the way to the city, he kept the radio going and all the news that came over it was bad. The storm was going to break records and motorists were advised to stay at home. Some of the parkways were already impassable, many trains were stalled and everywhere the drifts were tremendous. If it was bad now, what was it going to be like when Whitey had to take Mr. Blaster home?

Mr. Blaster did not believe a word the radio said. He acted as if the weather bureau had it in for him and was trying to tease and fluster him so that he wouldn't have his wits about him when he got to his office to close a big deal. "Big Deal" was Mr. Blaster's middle name. The only thing in the world he cared about was money and the only thing he liked to buy with it was more money.

He acted, too, as if Whitey was in cahoots with the weather people and was sliding around deliberately just to be a nuisance and make him late.

Finally, Whitey got sick and tired of Mr. Blaster's bad temper and he stopped. He could have gone on. He could easily have got to Wall Street, but he was angry now and decided to stand up for his rights. So he came to a full stop on a corner by a church.

He pretended to start again, but he really had no intention of doing so. Mr. Blaster flew into a roaring tantrum, the one that Elephi had seen and heard from his window. But Whitey did not care. All he wanted was to have a little peace and quiet and not have to listen another minute to that fat fault-finder. He was sure that Miss Alice would soon come to take him home.

Shortly after Mr. Blaster went stamping off, Whitey fell fast asleep. And he only woke up today, a few hours ago, when two men had come to dig him out of the snow.

"I don't know who they were," said Whitey. "And I don't know where I am. Do you know, Elephi?"

"Of course," said Elephi. "You're at my house," and he explained how he had seen

Whitey disappear and how he had brought about the rescue.

Whitey was greatly impressed. "Wow!" he said. "You do have *some* I.Q! And what do we do next?"

"First of all, are you hungry?" asked the hospitable cat.

"I don't think so," said Whitey, "but you might check my oil."

Since Elephi did not have the faintest idea how to do this but did not want to let Whitey see that there were gaps in his smartness, he changed the subject. He said, "I'm going to give you a bath."

With the first touch of Elephi's rough tongue, Whitey squeaked, "Hey, cut it out! You're tickling me!" but Elephi went right on in his quick, neat way and pretty soon Whitey admitted that it was rather fun to be cleaned by a cat.

When the worst of the spots and streaks were gone, Elephi lay down on Whitey's hood to rest and Whitey said, "Listen, you're a real friend. I'll never forget your kindness as long as I live.

But what's going to happen when your people
find me?"

"I don't know. I'll have to think about it,"
said Elephi. "They're nice. I think they'll in-
vite you to stay."

"But what about Miss Alice?" said Whitey. "She'll miss me and to tell you the honest truth, I miss her. I didn't care when I was asleep, but now . . ."

"Don't you want to stay with me?" asked Elephi forlornly. "We could box and wrestle and play hide-and-seek and things like that."

"Cars can't do things like that," said Whitey. "We can only play racing games and we can only do that out of doors."

"Oh," said Elephi. He fell silent in his disappointment and Whitey, taking pity on him, said, "Why don't you come live with us instead? You could go riding with Miss Alice and me."

Elephi shook his head. "I don't like the sound of Dandy Lion. He sounds too dumb. And the Cadillac sounds like a stuffed shirt. As for your Mr. Big Deal Blaster, I know I couldn't *stand* him."

Neither the cat nor the car could think of anything else to say.

In the silence, Elephi heard a key in the lock of the front door and he said, "Shhh! It's Mrs.

Cuckoo. I'll have to go now. I'll be back as soon as I can."

He yawned like a crocodile when he saw Mrs. Cuckoo and blinked his eyes and stretched as if he had just waked up from a long nap.

"That's not fair," said Mrs. Cuckoo. "All the time I've been in that killer's chair, you've been off in the Land of Nod."

She turned on the lamps and plumped up the cushions and as she picked up Elephi's own red one, she glanced out the window and said, "Why, the little white car is gone. I'm glad of that. It seemed unfriendly of its owners to leave it there all this time."

If you only knew where the white car is! thought Elephi. For the time being, he decided, it would be a good idea not to let Mrs. Cuckoo out of his sight. He knew it was going to be a shock to her when she found Whitey and he felt it would be easier when Mr. Cuckoo came home. So he followed her into the bedroom while she changed her shoes and combed her hair. And followed her into the kitchen while she prepared the tea tray. And followed her into the front hall when the doorbell rang. Mrs. Frenchman was there. (Mrs. Frenchman had another name but it was much too long and hard and since she was French, that's what Elephi called her.)

Elephi sat on a footstool near Mrs. Cuckoo as the ladies drank their tea and ate their macaroons and he listened to them talk of what they had bought for Christmas. Mrs. Cuckoo was going to give Mr. Cuckoo a clam steamer and a wheelbarrow to use next summer in the country. Mrs. Frenchman was going to give Mr. Frenchman a desk and a globe of the world.

"Do you have the clam steamer here?" asked Mrs. Frenchman. "I'd love to see it."

"Yes, it's here. Let me just fetch it from the back room," said Mrs. Cuckoo.

Oh, oh! Elephi's heart sank. He ran ahead of her and in the kitchen he rubbed against her legs and flicked his tail, pretending to be hungry, but she said to him, "Later, cat cat."

Sensibly Elephi hid in the cupboard where the paper towels were.

"What on earth!" exclaimed Mrs. Cuckoo, and she called, "Charlotte, come here!"

Mrs. Frenchman came to the back room on the double.

"What is it?" said Mrs. Cuckoo's friend.

"I'm not quite sure," said Mrs. Cuckoo. "But it distinctly looks like a car."

"For heaven's sake! It not only looks like a car, it most decidedly is one."

"And look," said Mrs. Cuckoo, "here's a tag addressed to us. But *how* did it get here?"

"You know, it really doesn't make sense," said Mrs. Frenchman.

"Nobody we know is rich enough to give us a car," said Mrs. Cuckoo. "And besides, we don't drive. I'm afraid it's a big mistake. A great big *fat* mistake that will get us into trouble."

"How do you mean into trouble?" said the French lady.

"Don't you imagine that it's been stolen?" And then, in a different tone of voice, she said, "Charlotte, do you know that I think this is that little bit of a car that stalled across the street several days ago? I noticed a while ago that it was gone."

How? Who? When? Mrs. Cuckoo and Mrs. Frenchman asked the questions over and over and then they began to laugh and when Mr. Cuckoo came home, he found them sitting on Whitey's hood laughing themselves silly.

Mr. Cuckoo called Walter and Walter said, "Why, yes, sir, it was settin' right there across the road, right there by the church, and seeing that it was addressed to you, me and Sam brought it up. Don't weigh no more than about like a big T.V. set."

"But how did you know it was there?" asked Mr. Cuckoo.

"Well, now, that was the funny part of it," said Walter, and Elephi, who was still hiding, imagined that he was scratching his head. "When your tom cat got out, I found him on top of this here little old car. Like he meant to lead me to it all along."

"No," said Mrs. Cuckoo. "It is well known that he's so smart he scares us, but not even Elephi could manage to steal a car for us."

"I don't know nothing about it," said Walter. "No more'n what I told you."

Walter left and the Cuckoos and Mrs. Frenchman went back into the living room to discuss how they should return Whitey to his rightful master. Elephi silently left his cupboard and went into Whitey's room. Somebody had opened Whitey's door and Elephi jumped in. "I didn't steal you," he whispered. "I rescued you!"

"I know it," said Whitey. "And it was the decentest thing a cat could do for a car. Tell me, though, Elephi, *why* did you do it?"

Elephi's eyes filled with tears. "Because I wanted a companion," he said. "And you looked about my age."

Whitey was solemn. "I know," he said. "I know what you mean. I've often felt the same way myself. Oh, Miss Alice is a peach and Dandy Lion is all right in his way. But it isn't much fun not to have a real pal."

"If they had asked another cat to come and live with us, I wouldn't have brought you here," said Elephi, "because now I see that it's not very comfortable for you in this room."

"To be perfectly frank, it isn't," said Whitey. "I feel cramped. I wish the vacuum cleaner would move over."

Mr. Cuckoo was at the telephone in the pantry calling the police and Elephi heard him say, "I can't explain it over the phone. Please send me an officer right away. Why can't I tell you? Because you wouldn't believe me, that's why. Oh, well, all right . . . there is a strange car in my apartment." There was a pause. "You heard me. I said there is a *strange car in my apartment.*"

Elephi said to Whitey, "Do you think they'll take me to jail?"

"Of course not," said Whitey and chuckled a little. "They'll never believe you did it. It's far more likely that they'll take the Cuckoos to jail."

"Oh, dear! I didn't mean to cause so much trouble," said poor Elephi.

"I hope somebody gets here soon," said Whitey. "Pressing against the wall like this makes my nose hurt. I'd like to sneeze but I'm afraid if I do I'll blow up."

Whenever Elephi was unhappy or whenever he had done something wrong or when he was faced with a problem that he could not solve, he found that the best policy was to go to sleep.

61

So he clasped his front paws over his eyes and purred a lullaby to himself and soon he was having his favorite dream of eating fresh catnip pie.

He was on his third helping of this imaginary treat when Whitey shook violently and hoarsely whispered, "The cops are here!"

Elephi had just time to get out of Whitey and to jump to a high shelf where he stood in a dark corner, half hidden by some boxes of moth balls.

Two large policemen, accompanied by Walter and Sam, the Cuckoos and Mrs. Frenchman, crowded around the doorway of the back room.

"So help me," said one of the policemen, a stout young man with red eyebrows and a red mustache to match. "So help me if you weren't telling the truth. Now let's hear the story."

Walter told his story again and Sam declared that this was exactly the way it all had happened. Both policemen wrote busily in their notebooks.

"We ought to take the lot of them to the station house," said the older of the two officers. "But I don't know what we could book them on."

"There must be some kind of a law against keeping a car in an apartment," said the younger. "But I never heard of it because I never heard of a car being in an apartment before."

"See if you can find any evidence in the glove compartment," said the first and the one with the red eyebrows began rooting about in Whitey's breast pocket.

"Yep, here we are," he said triumphantly as he withdrew a leather wallet full of papers. "Registered in the name of Miss Alice Blaster, Peppercorn Lake, New Rochelle." To Mr. Cuckoo, he said sternly, "Who is Miss Alice Blaster, Mister? And what is her car doing in your apartment?"

Mr. Cuckoo rubbed his hands together in despair. "I have never heard of Miss Alice Blaster and I would like to know why her car is here just as much as you would. I don't want her car. I don't want any car. I don't know how to drive and I don't intend to learn."

The young policeman gave him a hard look.

"Maybe you planned to sell this stolen goods?" he said. "Is that your racket?"

The other policeman said, "Ease up, Murphy. I think the guy is telling the truth. Let's call the boss and see what we ought to do next."

Murphy went to the pantry to telephone and came back with the news that a Mr. Blaster had reported a missing car. A white Fiat that he had left by the Presbyterian church in the great snow. He had gone to haul it out this afternoon and, when he found that it was not there, he had looked for it first at the car pound and then had appealed to the police. He was being notified at his house in New Rochelle.

For the time being, nothing more could be done and Mrs. Cuckoo suggested that everyone go into the living room and be comfortable while waiting for Mr. Blaster's call.

"Oh, I *wish* they'd hurry," moaned Whitey. "I'm smothering! I'm hot! Every part of me hurts!"

"I'm sorry," said Elephi from his perch.

"Oh, I don't blame you," said Whitey. "You

65

meant well. But I think that for a cat with such a high I.Q. you should have figured out that these quarters would be too snug for me."

Elephi knew he deserved the scolding, but all the same it broke his heart.

"You might teach me how to purr," said Whitey. "It would help pass the time."

Once again Elephi made a circle of himself on Whitey's hood and began to demonstrate the principles of purring.

Just as Whitey was beginning to get the hang of it, the policemen and the Cuckoos and Mrs. Frenchman came trooping back. And with them was a very pretty girl in a tall fur hat.

"Yes, it certainly *is* my car!" cried the girl and rushed to pat Whitey's head. Elephi gathered from the general conversation that Miss Alice was staying in the city for a few days and her father had telephoned from New Rochelle to tell her where she could find Whitey.

"It's such a faithful little car," she said, smiling and rubbing a bit of smudge off Whitey's windshield with a handkerchief that smelled

66

of violets. "I don't care how it got here. I think it was rather a sweet mistake."

"I'm glad you do," said Mrs. Cuckoo, greatly relieved.

Miss Alice laughed. "It's a good thing I was in town. I don't think Daddy would think it was such a sweet mistake."

"You don't want to press any charges against these people, then, is that it?" asked Murphy.

"Certainly not," said Miss Alice. "I think it's an awfully funny joke. The question is, how am I going to get the cute little thing out of here?"

"We'll get it out the way it got in," said Mr. Cuckoo, "and the quicker the better," and he went off to ring the bell of the service elevator to summon Walter. "Walter has been called umpteen times today. Think what I'm going to have to tip him!"

Policeman Murphy said, "Okay, maybe you got a better idea? Maybe you'd like to buy it from Miss Blaster and leave it here? Some peculiar interior decorating that would be, I must say."

"How ridiculous it all is," said Mrs. Cuckoo.

"How impossible," said Mrs. Frenchman.

"How *funny!*" said Miss Blaster.

The service elevator was out of order. According to Walter it had just up and died on him and it would be days before it could be repaired.

Whitey was too big for the front elevator.

The Cuckoos groaned.

The policemen grew impatient.

Miss Alice stopped laughing and began to cry.

The story is now well known of how, at dinner time the night before Christmas eve in the year of the historic snowstorm, an emergency squad of workmen swarmed into the building on lower Fifth Avenue to remove a car.

The news of this amazing event spread quickly and so many curious people gathered on the sidewalk out front that special policemen were sent over to direct traffic.

"You say they're taking a car out?" said newcomers to the scene.

"I'm not sure whether it's a car or a *cow*," they were told.

The doormen from the apartment houses and the hotels down the avenue came to watch. The Presbyterian minister stared from the doorway of the church and his bell ringer forgot to ring the bell at half past five. Everyone, including the workmen, was very jolly. It was agreed that this was the most outlandish thing that had ever happened in this part of town and possibly the most outlandish thing anywhere ever.

The crowd was delighted when they saw a huge net being raised by pulleys up the side of the building and a great cheer went up when Whitey's nose appeared in Elephi's bay window.

"I *said* it was a car, not a cow," said somebody. "What would a cow be doing in a New York City apartment?"

As the basket with Whitey in it slowly, ever so slowly, descended, the crowd moved back, not wanting to get bumped on the head.

"Bravo!"

"Hurray!"

"Well done!"

"Did you ever!"

"Well I never!"

There was only one heavy heart among all those people, and it belonged to Elephi.

"Goodbye, Whitey," called Elephi as the car disappeared over the window ledge.

"So long, Elephi," said Whitey. "No hard feelings. You were a brick to do what you did even though it didn't turn out right. And thanks for the purring lesson."

"Don't mention it," said Elephi. "And remember what I told you. Proper purring depends on proper breathing."

The Well-Known Cat leaned out the window as far as he dared and watched the people gather around Whitey. Newspaper reporters and photographers interviewed Miss Alice and took pictures of her and her car. They came up to the Cuckoos' apartment and photographed the room where Whitey had been found. They wrote down Walter's story in detail.

"What a story!" they said.

"Scoop!" they said.

They said, "This takes the cake!"

Late into the night, the Cuckoos talked about their adventure. Sometimes they shook their heads in disbelief and sometimes they laughed until their stomachs ached.

Elephi did not think it was a laughing matter.

His first and only friend was gone.

Poor Cat!

The next evening before dinner, Mrs. Cuckoo said to Mr. Cuckoo, "The dentist hurts me."

"He wouldn't be a good dentist if he didn't hurt," said Mr. Cuckoo. "You should try to think about other things when you're in his chair."

"I do," said Well Known's friend. "Today I was thinking about the white car. I *know* Elephi had something to do with it. I don't know what, but something . . . the way he was curled up on the seat when Miss Blaster came . . . the way Walter found it to begin with."

"Supposing he did have something to do with it," said Mr. Cuckoo. "Why would he want a Fiat for a toy?"

"I don't think he wants a toy exactly," said Mrs. C., "I think he wants a companion."

"That's cuckoo," said Mr. Cuckoo.

"Why cuckoo?" she asked. "All young creatures need playmates."

"Well," said Mr. Cuckoo, weakening, "Well . . ."

"I'll tell you what," said Mrs. Cuckoo. "This afternoon as I was waiting for the bus, two Presbyterian children with their older sister stopped to show me a picture one of them had made. I couldn't tell what it was meant to be and so I asked. They told me it was a mother cat with four kittens."

"Mmmm," said Mr. Cuckoo and rattled his newspaper.

"So naturally I inquired."

"Naturally."

"The kittens are six weeks old," said Mrs. Cuckoo. "Their mother is a silver tabby and their father is a black Persian."

"Yes?"

"The Presbyterian children said they would give me one for Christmas."

"I'm sure they would."

"Oh, please! It would make Elephi so happy!"

"All right, all right," said Mr. Cuckoo. "Can't have an unhappy cat around the house. Where is the rogue, by the way?"

The rogue came out from behind a row of rare books and knocked several of them onto the floor.

"I know you stole that car," said Mrs. Cuckoo, "but how did you manage to do it?"

"Are you sure he wants a Presbyterian kitten?" asked her husband.

Elephi answered in this way: he purred thunderously. He chased his tail with joy. He boxed the curtain pull, getting into practice for sparring matches. He sprinted down the hall, pawed his personal walnut, yanked up a window shade, found the green rubber birthday mouse and chewed its ear smack off.

The savage cat, as fearless as a lion, dragged the mouse by the tail and laid it at Mr. Cuckoo's feet.

"Thank you, Elephi," said Mr. Cuckoo. "May I keep this mouse? Or is it only on loan?"

"He can have the kitten, can't he?"

"He can have the kitten if I can have this excellent green rubber mouse," said Mr. Cuckoo.

Suddenly Elephi was so tired that he had to lie down. He had been working hard the last few days and he needed a good long sleep.

The last thing he heard, before Mr. Sandman came to take him to the Land of Nod, was Mrs. Cuckoo saying, "I daresay you realize that I accepted the kitten without asking you if I could. The children are bringing him first thing in the morning."

Oh, goody!

Games!

Secrets!
But right now:
Snooze.